# WHAT WE'LL BUILD

PLANS FOR OUR TOGETHER FUTURE

OLIVER JEFFERS

HarperCollins *Children's Books*

What shall we build, you

*To my daughter, Mari* (and Granny Marie)

We have much to do.

First published in hardback in Great Britain by HarperCollins *Children's Books* in 2020

1 3 5 7 9 10 8 6 4 2

ISBN: 978-0-00-838220-9

HarperCollins *Children's Books* is a division of HarperCollins*Publishers* Ltd.
Text and illustrations copyright © Oliver Jeffers 2020
Design: Rory Jeffers
Page 8 pencil lettering based on a quote from
*Richelieu; Or, The Conspiracy* by Edward Bulwer-Lytton, 1839

The author/illustrator asserts the moral right to be identified as the author/illustrator of the work.

Visit our website at: www.harpercollins.co.uk

Printed in China

*You are only free to dream and plan (for the future)
when you are not battling to survive (the present).
To all those fathers and daughters on this orb whose odds are
stacked less fortuitously than ours, our aim is to even the field.
Love, Oliver and Mari*

**In remembrance of Óscar and Valeria,
who tried and never made it across**

and I?

Let's gather all our tools for a start.

For putting together

and taking apart.

Let's build a door

where there was none.

We'll build a house

to be our home.

We'll build a watch to keep our time.

We'll build some love to set aside,

and build a hole where we can hide.

A fortress to keep
our enemies out,

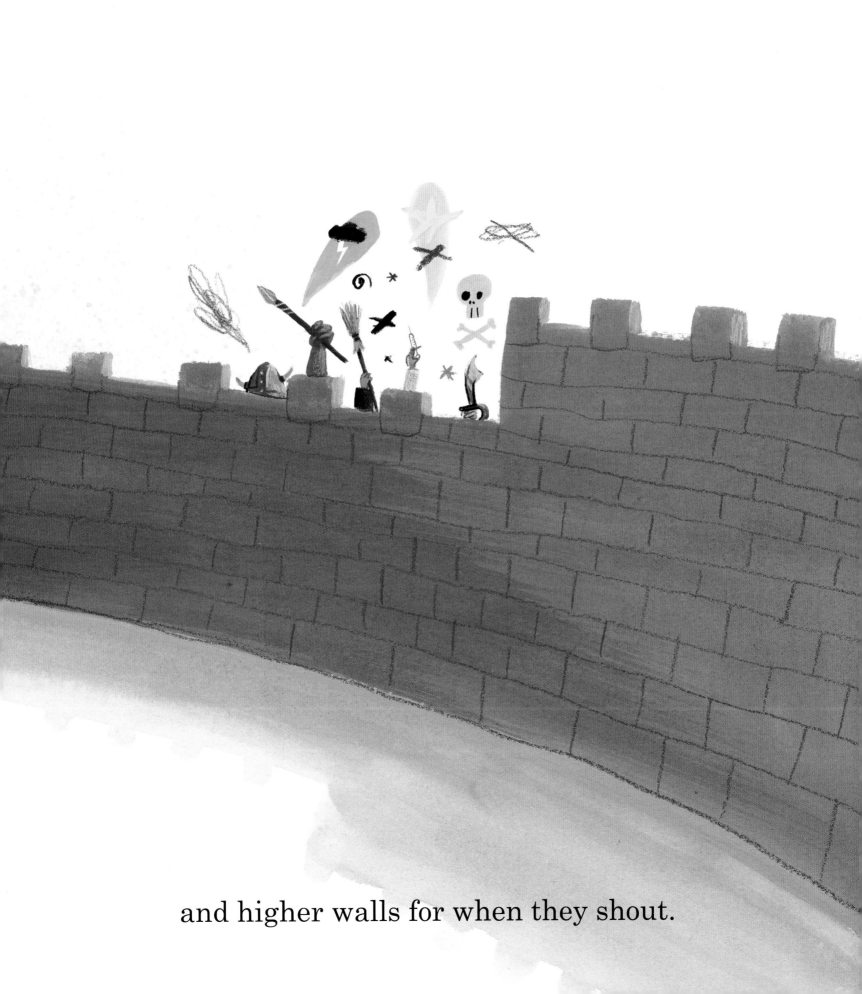

and higher walls for when they shout.

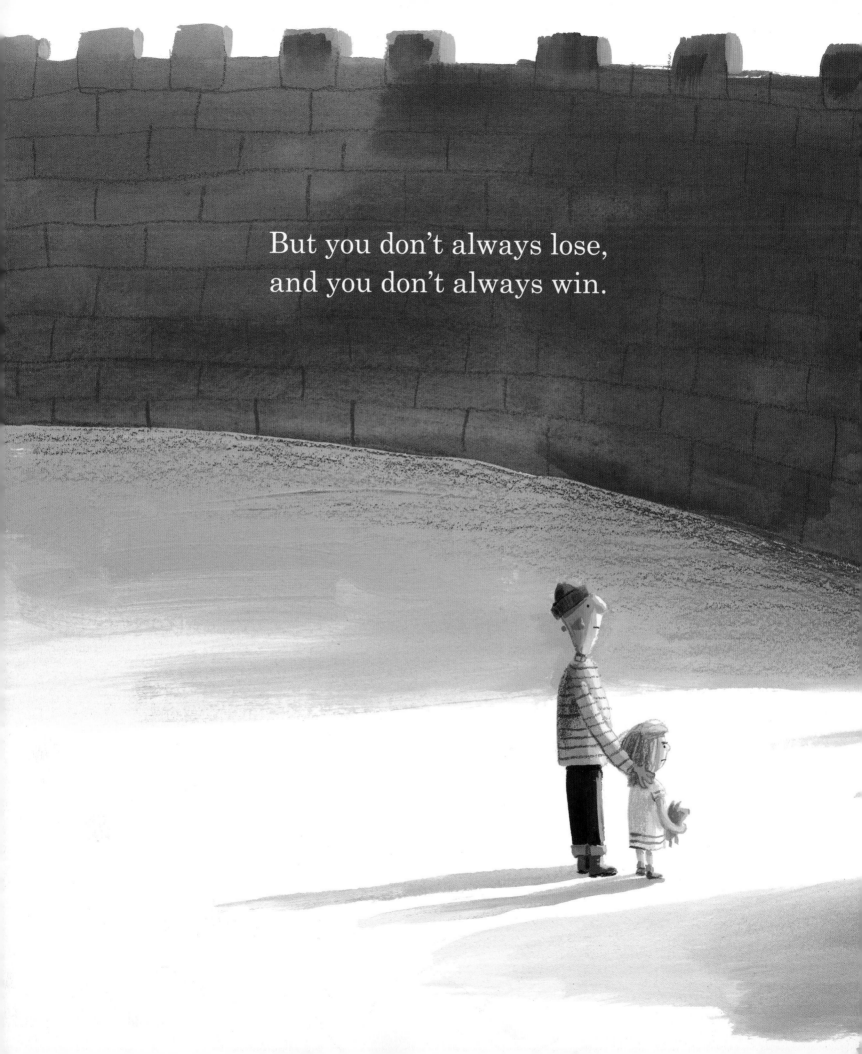

But you don't always lose,
and you don't always win.

So we'll build a gate to let them in.

We'll build a table to drink our tea,
and say...

We'll build a tower
to watch the sky,

and other worlds
that pass us by.

Let's build a tunnel to anywhere.

Let's build a road up to the moon.

Let's build a comfy place to rest,
for we'll be tired soon.

Let's build a boat that can't be broken.

that will not sink, or be cracked open.

A place to stay when all is lost,

to keep the things we love the most.

We'll put these favourite things beside

the earlier love we set aside.

I think that we may want them later,

when times are hard and needs are greater.

But, first things first, let's build a fire,

for we've planned a lot and now we're tired.

It'll keep us warm like when we're born,

then we'll say good night, as all's all right.

These are the things
we'll build,

you and I.